The Prince's Secret

A Thrilling Medieval Gay Romance

By Candace Young

Disclaimer:
This is a work of fiction. Names, characters, businesses, places, events, locales, and incidents are either the products of the author's imagination or used in a fictitious manner. Any resemblance to actual persons, living or dead, or actual events is purely coincidental. Author disclaim any liability to any party for any loss, damage, or disruption caused by errors or omissions, whether such errors or omissions result from negligence, accident, or any other cause from this book.

Copyright:
In no way is it legal to reproduce, duplicate, or transmit any part of this document in either electronic means or in printed format. Recording of this publication is strictly prohibited and any storage of this document is not allowed unless with written permission from the publisher. All rights reserved.

The information provided herein is stated to be truthful and consistent, in that any liability, in terms of inattention or otherwise, by any usage or abuse of any policies, processes, or directions contained within is the solitary and utter responsibility of the recipient reader. Under no circumstances will any legal responsibility or blame be held against the publisher for any reparation, damages, or monetary loss due to the information herein, either directly or indirectly.

Respective authors own all copyrights not held by the publisher. The information herein is offered for informational purposes solely, and is universal as so. The presentation of the information is without contract or any type of guarantee assurance.

The trademarks that are used are without any consent, and the publication of the trademark is without permission or backing by the trademark owner. All trademarks and brands within this book are for clarifying purposes only and are the owned by the owners themselves, not affiliated with this document

Table of Contents

Chapter 1	4
Chapter 2	19
Chapter 3	28
Chapter 4	35

Chapter 1

At night, Prince Cassius almost felt as though he could be himself. He was still watched by a few guards and a servant could poke his head into the room at any time, but he was no longer under the constant eye of his parents and other nobles. He didn't have to talk like he was giving a speech or stand up straight enough to balance books on his head. He could change into his most comfortable attire and sit on his balcony, looking over the castle walls and out into town. It the closest to independence a Prince could really hope for.

Normally Cassius would sit in silence, but today had been especially rough. He leaned back against the door and spoke out into the void of the darkness.

"Today was not a good day," he said. It felt good just to say something, to say anything. He didn't get to speak his mind very often. "I think I may have messed everything up."

Really Cassius didn't just think he had messed up. He knew that he had. The look of anger on his father's face as he spoke to the court had been enough to prove that something was wrong, and Cassius was not foolish enough to think it could be about something else. He had made a gamble, and now his father's Kingdom would have to pay for it.

Cassius leaned his head up against the door to look up at the sky. It was a cloudy night, and he couldn't see any stars. He wished he could. He always found comfort in their tiny lights.

He sighed. "I just wish I could have more than one chance to get things right. I wish I didn't have to be the one to make all these decisions."

Something on the ground rustled in the wind. Cassius smiled at the small disturbance. At least the animals in the castle garden were on his side.

"I would fix it if I could," he said. "It's just the only way to fix it at this point... well, my father thinks I should marry this Noblewoman from their Kingdom. Forge ties and all that. Fix whatever rift I tried to tear open. But I don't even like--"

Cassius was cut off by a thud from the other side of his balcony. He startled and instinctively tried to move away from the noise. His back was already against his doorway, so he didn't get far. He looked to the source of the sound and was surprised to see a man of about his age in a heap near the railing.

"Who are you?" Cassius demanded. He scrambled to his feet and his hand reached for a sword that wasn't there. He hadn't thought he would need one on his personal balcony.

The heap of a person stood. Cassius noticed for the first time that he was wearing a knight's uniform. Whoever had just climbed onto his balcony was under the employ of his father.

"Hi," the man said. He ran a hand through his unruly hair. He still hadn't looked up at Cassius. "Sorry for the abrupt introduction, but--"

His words got stuck in his throat as he looked up and saw Cassius. "Wait... you're the prince."

Cassius nodded. "Yes. What are you doing on my balcony? How did you even get here?

"I'm so sorry Prince Cassius," the knight lowered himself into a bow. "I didn't realize this was your balcony. I just heard someone in distress and I thought perhaps I could offer reassurance."

"Is that so?" Cassius challenged.

"Yes," the knight said. "I should never have climbed up here, I'm so sorry."

He started to step back over the railing.

"Wait!" Cassius demanded. "You weren't sent by my father?"

"No," the knight said. He sounded serious. "I left my post to come here. I very well may lose my knighthood if your father finds out."

"I won't tell him," Cassius said. "But please stay. I could use company that was not sent by my father."

Cassius didn't really know why he asked the guard to stay. He told himself it was to get away from the influence of his father, but the way his eyes kept lingering on the man's lips made it seem as though it may have been something else entirely.

The guard was under his family's employ, and Cassius' suggestion was not one he could easily deny. He sat down with his back to the railing so that he faced Cassius. Even from a distance, Cassius could make out the blue of his eyes.

"I'm sorry to keep you away from you post," Cassius said. Already he wondered if inviting the man to stay was a huge mistake. It was certainly a temptation.

"I'm only meant to protect you," the guard said. "I can do that as easily from here as anywhere else."

The knight did not seem engaged in the conversation. Cassius wondered if he had some sort of walls up that prevented him from talking freely. He wondered if some of those walls came from his own position of power.

"What is your name?" he asked, trying to spark a conversation.

"I'm Lucas," he said. He didn't add anything more.

Cassius leaned his head back again, ready to give up and send the knight back to where he had come from.

"What were you upset about?" Lucas asked suddenly. "I would have thought Prince would be a pretty sweet gig."

"It can be," Cassius said. "And I generally like it, it's just... well I have to make these big decisions that effect everyone and this time I chose wrong."

"I'm sure you didn't make the wrong choice," Lucas said.

"You won't be saying that in a month when we're at war."

Lucas turned to sit next to Cassius instead of across from him. He set a gentle hand on Cassius' leg. "I'm sure you did the best you could."

Lucas seemed to open up a bit more after that. He was reassuring, but honest in a refreshing way. Cassius was able to talk to him without policing his own words and he felt like Lucas was starting to do the same. With each laugh and shift in conversation they drew a little closer together, both physically and mentally. It was not until nearly dawn that the young knight had to leave, and by this point they had found many things to connect over. Cassius was sorry to see him go.

"Let me know if you run into any trouble with my father," he said. "I can take care of it."

"I will," Lucas said. "It was nice to talk to you. I never knew our crown prince was so... human."

They paused, and a feeling lingered in the air between them. Neither seemed willing to put a voice to it. Finally, Cassius spoke up.

"I'm up here nearly every night," he said. "If you have a chance, I'd love to do this again."

Lucas smiled. "I would too. I'll see what I can do."

He stepped over the balcony and ducked out of sight. Cassius tried to ignore the racing of his heart, but it was no use. He knew what he was feeling. He knew what he wanted.

Cassius was playing as dangerous a game with his heart as he was his kingdom.

Chapter 2

Cassius tried not to get his hopes up about Lucas. He reminded himself that the knight may not even want to meet up again, and that even if he did he may not have the same things in mind. That night he spent his time on the balcony pacing back and forth, stopping at every rustle from below to listen more closely. As the night grew late, he gave up on his ambitions and sat back down. He should not have expected Lucas to join him. He had let his hopes get ahead of him.

But then, almost as if in response to Cassius' despondence, there was movement along the rail. Lucas appeared bit by bit until he was over the rail. Cassius stood and went to him.

"You came," he greeted with a nod.

"I thought I owed it to my country," Lucas said with a smile to show he was only joking. Still, Cassius felt as though he needed to make one thing abundantly clear.

"You know that you're free to go," he said. "I want you here as a friend, not as an obedient subject."

"I know," Lucas said. "I was only joking."

"Good," Cassius said.

Again they sat and again they talked and again Cassius' eyes were drawn to Lucas' lips. They talked about everything and when there was nothing more to talk about they talked about the stars.

"I don't like cloudy nights," Cassius said. "I like looking out on the stars. I like know there's something out there that my father can't control, can't even reach."

Lucas looked to the sky. "Your father can't control the clouds either."

"No," Cassius said. "But clouds are perhaps nothing more than an omen of worse things. Stars... they're just beautiful. No reasoning, no apology, no expectations."

"Kind of like you," Lucas said. "Absolutely beautiful."

Cassius didn't know what came over him, but at the sound of the compliment he found himself leaning in. He pressed a gentle kiss against Lucas' lips, and if felt as though spark flew. It was a moment of pure bliss, broken only by the first drops of rain from the storm that had been blowing in all week.

The water awoke Cassius to what he had done. He panicked a bit and searched Lucas' face for any sight of emotion. He had never felt so foolish in his life.

"I'm so sorry," he said. "I really shouldn't have done that. You were just complimenting me and you're so handsome and..."

Cassius trailed off. He realized he wasn't making anything better. The first few raindrop had given way into a heavy rain and it made everything worse. Now he could not even invite Lucas inside to get out of the rain without it sounding like he was suggesting something more. He turned his eyes to the ground. If there had been any emotion worth seeing in Lucas' face he would have seen it by now.

He felt a hand graze his waist. He saw Lucas' boots move forward a step. He felt the Lucas' hand on his cheek as his head was tilted upwards. Then, best of all, he felt Lucas' lips against his own.

They kissed in the pouring rain, and when he had to pull away for breath, Lucas said: "Don't be sorry."

The rain glued their skin to their bodies and their passions glued their bodies to one another. Cassius felt free for the first time in his life and he allowed his hands to explore Lucas' body with abandon. Lucas returned the enthusiasm by pushing Cassius backwards. For just a moment he was pressed against a closed door, but the latch didn't hold and they both tumbled into his room. Lucas landed on top of Cassius, and for a moment he paused to smile down at the prince. Then his hand reached under Cassius shirt and started to pull it off of him. No one had ever taken anything from Cassius before. He enjoyed not being the one in control for once, and he gave himself over to Lucas entirely.

For the first time in a very long time, Cassius didn't spare a single thought for his kingdom. he thought only of the way Lucas' body felt against his and the warmth of a shared bed.

Chapter 3

Cassius and Lucas met up nearly every night. Some nights they repeated the spectacle from their second night together, exploring each other with a passion unrivaled in Cassius' previous pursuits. Many nights they merely spoke to one another. Cassius enjoyed the conversation without pressure or expectations, and he found that Lucas was a genuinely good man as well as a good soldier. They were blissfully happy as a couple, living outside of the political world.

At least until Cassius was introduced to Esmeralda Hoffman. She was a distinguished noblewoman with carefully traced ancestry. She was snooty and unkind and far older than Cassius, but his father still expected him to show interest. A few months ago, this would hardly have been a problem-- nearly every emotion Cassius displayed in public was to some degree a fake, and attraction would have been an easy one. But it just so happened that on the day that Cassius' father introduced Cassius to Esmeralda, Lucas was a part of the guard detail. Cassius could hardly bear to express false affection under the eye of his genuine lover.

"Prince Cassius," Esmeralda greeted with a curtsy. "It's wonderful to meet you."

"You as well," Cassius greeted. He bowed deeper than he ought to have and tried to ignore Lucas' eyes on his back. "You look lovely today."

"I would hope that you thought so, given your father's intention for us," she said.

"My father's intentions?" Cassius looked up at his father. "What might those be?"

"Do you remember when your kingdom attempted to encroach on ours? That first land your seized along our northern border belonged to my family. Your father intends to make it right through a prosperous marriage."

Cassius remembered now his father's pleas that he take a scorned noblewoman as his wife. He out to have connected the dots far sooner, but with Lucas on his mind a romance to another was far from what he sought. He could not imagine what Lucas was feeling, trapped in his position by the door and unable to contribute.

"That does sound very..." Cassius searched for the right word. "Diplomatic."

"You're a Prince, dear," Esmeralda said. "That's all your marriage is going to be."

The idea of marrying Lucas had not crossed Cassius' mind before, and it only did so now as an impossibility. He had lingered in the present moment to enjoy the bliss of their relationship, and here he was yet again with his position holding him back. He could not even conceptualize a future where he could live happily with Lucas. Even if his father approved of Cassius' attraction towards men, a marriage to Lucas would lack any diplomatic advantage. As long as Cassius was a prince, he could not have a future with Lucas.

It stung.

"While it's very nice to meet you, I'm afraid I'm feeling unwell. Perhaps we can talk another time," Cassius said.

He hurried out of the room. He could feel them all watching him, from Esmeralda to his father to Lucas. He just wished he could stop watching. He just wished he could be someone other than the prince for once.

Chapter 4

He almost didn't want to see Lucas that night. There was a lot on his mind, but Lucas remained at the front of it. He knew talking was meant to be helpful, but he couldn't think of anything to say that would fix things.

Lucas didn't look happy when he appeared over the railing. That only made Cassius feel worse.

Silently, Lucas sat down next to him. He set a gentle hand on Cassius' leg in the same way he had on the night they had met.

""I know you have to marry her," Lucas said.

Cassius looked away. He didn't want to talk about it.

"Look, I saw the way you were posturing for me in there. It's okay. I can handle it. I know that you're a prince and your marriage is important. I know you have to marry her," Lucas said.

"I don't want to," Cassius said.

"I know," Lucas told him. "But it's what the prince does. It's what you have to do."

"I wish I didn't," Cassius said. "I wish..."

He trailed off. There were a million things he wished, but many he could not voice for fear. He had only bee with Lucas for a few months. He didn't want to scare the man away. Still his mind went to happy domestic scenes that included them both. He could see a future between them, but it was not as fate had intended.

In the pictures of his perfect future, Cassius was not a prince. Really that was what it all came back to: his royalty. If there was merely a way for him to cast it aside, he would do so in an instant.

And then, Cassius realized that he could.

Were he willing to sacrifice everything he had ever been given, he could abdicate his claim on the throne. He run from the castle without looking back. He could run away from his title and responsibilities hand in hand with Lucas and play out every scenario that haunted his mind.

"Wishing is for cowards and laymen," he said. "Let's make this a reality."

"Make what a reality?" Lucas asked.

"I'm abdicating my right to the crown," Cassius said. "I'm stepping away from a marriage I don't want and a life I don't want."

"Are you sure?" Lucas asked, looking more serious than Cassius had ever seen him.

"I've never been more sure of anything in my life," Cassius said.

Lucas smiled and took his hand. They marched down the hall to Cassius' father. Cassius explained everything and expressed his intention to abdicate the crown. His father expressed little remorse. Cassius' older cousin would make a wonderful match for Esmeralda and was far more suited for the crown than Cassius.

When Cassius stepped outside the castle, he was no longer a prince. He walked away from his castle hand in hand with his lover.

It was not quite riding into the sunset, but it felt like it to Cassius. It felt like the perfect fairy tale ending.

Made in the USA
Columbia, SC
06 February 2021